Other titles
by the author

Big Little Voice

DRIES MY TEARS

By M.G. Vaciago

Illustrated by Glen Holman

Matador
Unit E2 Airfield Business Park,
Harrison Road, Market Harborough,
Leicestershire. LE16 7UL
Tel: 0116 2792299
Email: books@troubador.co.uk
Web: www.troubador.co.uk/matador
Twitter: @matadorbooks

ISBN 978 1803132 266

British Library Cataloguing in Publication Data.
A catalogue record for this book is available from the British Library.

Printed and bound by CPI Group (UK) Ltd, Croydon, CR0 4YY
Typeset in 20pt Blockhead OT by Troubador Publishing Ltd, Leicester, UK

Matador is an imprint of Troubador Publishing Ltd

Dedicated to my dad

I miss you

x

My Friday evenings are
so full of dread,

When all my friends are
excited instead.

Eagerly awaiting two
days of no school;

For them it's a joy, but
for me it's just cruel.

I lie on my bed and I quietly sob;

My eyes start to sting and my
head starts to throb.

Where did you go? and
why did you leave?

I miss you more than
you'd ever believe.

My weekends were filled
with endless joy,

Adventures we'd share and
trips we'd enjoy.

So much laughter that my
sides would get sore,

When at your bad jokes,
together we'd roar.

Now it's all different and
I dread the weekend,

I just sit in my room and
wish it would end.

I can't see a way out of
all this grey,

And my mood just gets darker,
day after day.

A few weeks ago, our lives were rocked,

Although it was expected, we were all still shocked.

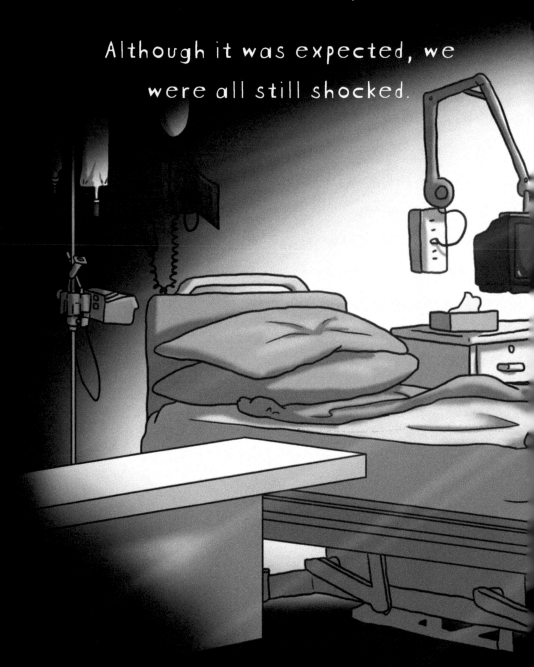

You took your last
breath and then
slipped away,

And I've been
stuck in a daze
since that sad day.

Over the months we saw
you waste away,

Deteriorating somehow every day.

Becoming weaker, till you could
no longer stand,

All we could do was sit and
hold your hand.

After school, I'd sit with
you every day,

And quietly in my head I would pray.

That I wouldn't lose you and
you'd stay with me,

But it was painfully clear,
that it wasn't to be.

My mum would cry because
your time was brief,

And we were already feeling
overwhelming grief.

Then one day, she said
you were gone,

And life would be different,
from then on.

Arrangements were made for
your final goodbye,

I chose to attend but I'm confused
about why.

I don't understand what I thought
I'd achieve,

But I really missed you and didn't
want you to leave.

There we stood around
your grave,

Mourning the life we
could not save.

You fought so hard; you fought for so long;

You were so brave; you were so very strong.

We walked away from you in
floods of tears,

Leaving the person we'd loved
through the years.

1940–2019
LOVING HUSBAND, FATHER
AND GRANDAD

WE MISS YOU

You were my grandad, my
hero, my friend,

Someone whom I loved always,
without end.

I wish things had been different and
you could've stayed;

I miss you so much, it gets
worse every day.

I know you were suffering
and you were in pain,

And ultimately our loss is
heaven's gain.

Come back for one night, just
to say goodbye?

I promise I won't make a fuss
and won't cry,

When you have to leave,
when it's time.

I just want to see you, as you
were, in your prime.

17

I want to remember you
laughing out loud,

When being my gramps made
you so very proud.

Not as I saw you last, gaunt
and in pain,

Even though you smiled and
didn't complain.

What do I do now? You were my
go-to, my friend.

I could always be honest, and on
you I could depend.

I love my parents dearly but it
was different with you,

We were always together and
stuck like glue.

The memories we shared are now
just videos and stills,

Lining the bookcases and
our window sills.

I see you, but can't hug you,
or share an embrace,

I feel lost and uncertain,
alone in this place.

I still can't believe
you're really gone,

I'm struggling to stand
up and carry on.

I still expect you to walk
through the door,

But that won't happen, as
you are no more.

That night, as I lay down in my bed,

A glimmer of me appeared
over my head.

"Don't be afraid," the voice
said soft and low;

It was the me I remembered
from years ago.

"My dear friend," the voice said,
"I see your pain,

And for that reason, I've
come back once again.

To remind you that life doesn't end
when someone goes,

They leave this world for a
place no one knows."

"Tell me your thoughts and all
of your fears,

No need to hide your pain
and your tears.

To make sense of your feelings,
you have to be true,

So, tell me honestly what's happening
inside of you?"

"I can't explain how I feel inside.

To make sense of it all, I've
really tried.

Of how I feel, I've never
really spoken,

But all I know is I'm totally
heartbroken."

"I'm angry that he fell ill
and got so sick,

I'm shocked that he was taken
from me so quick.

I feel lost because he was
my best friend,

Someone who'd never judge and on
whom I could depend."

"I'm sad about all the games we
didn't get to play,

And all the things I didn't get to say.

I'm upset my achievements he'll
never get to see,

And the adult that I'll grow up to be."

"There are so many things I
don't understand,

And he was always the person
to take my hand,

And help guide my thoughts,
when I'm lost in a maze.

He was a very wise man, in so
many ways."

"Your grandad is a person you'll
never forget,

Life forces you to carry on, and yet,

He'll always be with you,
driving you on.

His body has left, but his
spirit's not gone."

"What if he gets to heaven and
there's no more space?

All the room taken up and he
hasn't got a place.

What will happen and
where will he go?

It's all so confusing, and
I just need to know."

"Someone once told me, when
we're born a room is set aside,

And when we go to heaven,
that door opens wide.

No one is sure what happens when
life forces us apart,

Except that they'll always live, in
a space within our heart."

"Death takes a person away, but
never the life they had.

Those memories are yours to unlock
whenever you're feeling sad.

The fun you had together is in your
life's history book,

It's always there for you to see,
so let's go take a look."

"Let's take a trip to a place
from the past;

Although he is gone, the
memories last.

Hold my small hand as we travel,
through time and space,

To a place full of happiness, that
death can't erase."

"Do you remember this place, the
trees and the lake?

When after school, trips
together you'd take:

Feeding the ducks and flying a kite,

Running down the hill so it
would take flight?"

"Yes, I remember it well; my grandad would say:

'Come on, old kite, fly up and away'.

We'd run and we'd run, laughing with glee,

As it would take off and then crash into a tree."

"We would sit on a bench and make extravagant schemes,

Of how we would realise our ultimate dreams,

Of being adventurers and finding lost treasure,

Then living a life of permanent leisure."

"Our trips to the park would
be so much fun,

When I'd scoot ahead and behind
me, he'd run.

The ice-cream we'd buy was so
gooey and thick,

And we'd laugh when to his face,
the sprinkles would stick."

"Why am I laughing? Grandad
is gone,

It's so disrespectful and so
very wrong.

No one talks anymore so I'm
alone in this land,

With feelings of loss that
I don't understand."

"Please take me home, I don't
want to stay.

I've refused to come here
since he passed away.

This place is a reminder that
he is now gone,

And park trips won't be the
same from now on."

"The kite's thrown in the box and
now full of dust,

But fly it again, you have
to, you must.

It will bring back the memories
you stored away,

And your grandad will be
with you, as you play."

"By trying to ignore the memories
you have in your heart,

You are pushing your bond
to him further apart.

Instead, what you really must do,

Is bring his memory even
closer to you."

"Create a haven for yourself,
a place you can go,

Any time you feel sad, a
little lost or low.

Fill this space with keepsakes and
things that make you smile,

Think of your grandad and stay
there a while."

"Fill a box with photos, trinkets and
things that you shared,

It may make you cry in the beginning,
but don't be scared.

As time moves on, you'll find comfort
in memories you made,

The loss will never go away, but the
pain may start to fade."

"Come on, let's make a start and make a special box,

You can add a photo, if you like, or some of those painted rocks.

The ones you found in the park, hidden in a tree trunk.

Grandad said to toss them out as they were worthless junk."

I laugh out loud, as I remember the scene,

As I picked it up and wiped it clean.

It was a kindness rock and not one to throw,

I gave it to Grandad and said, "There you go!"

"What's this for?" he said as he
looked at it closely,

At the picture on the back and then
back to me.

"It says 'never apart', with two
hearts entwined,

One heart is yours and the
other is mine."

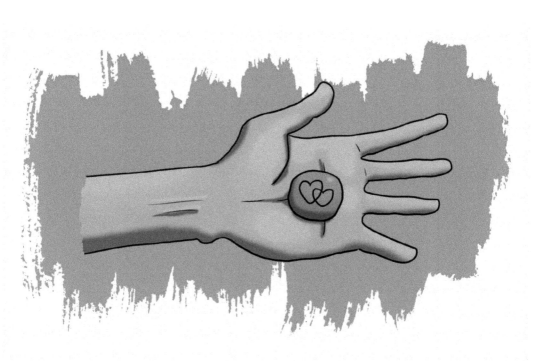

"Jack, keep this rock safe
and guard it well,

It's magic and within it,
memories dwell.

In time you'll hold it and remember
this place,

I hope it brings comfort and a
smile to your face."

With a photo here and a
postcard there,

I've boxed up the life that
we did share.

Reminding me of all we did together;

This is a box I'll treasure forever.

The box is soon full of pictures
and souvenirs,

That Grandad and I collected over
the years.

It made me feel Grandad was
alive and still here,

But when I closed the lid,
I shed a tear.

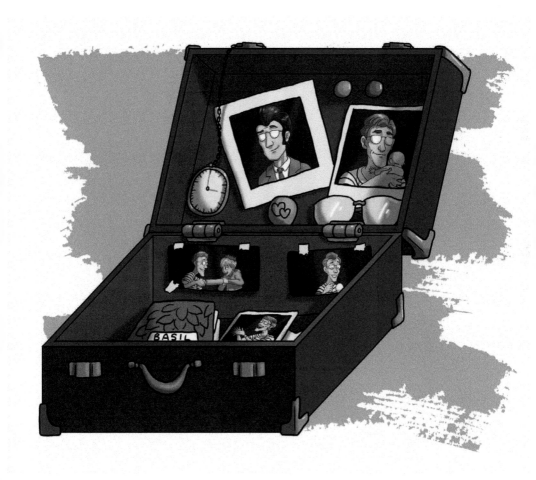

"You must confess to someone
about your grief,

Get it out in the open,
it'll be a relief.

That's the first step to moving on;

It doesn't mean he'll be forgotten
or that he's gone."

"Your mum tries to talk, but she's not
getting through;

Do you not see, she's grieving
just like you?

She smiles through the tears
she's fighting to hide,

And her grief is ripping her apart
from inside."

"Grief is something you share,
your common ground,

And a way of moving forward will
somehow be found,

But take the first step and acknowledge
what's true,

And find a way to help each
other through."

"I don't know what to do or
how I should be,

I've never lost anyone that
close to me.

Am I allowed to laugh or to even smile?

Or am I supposed to be quiet and
sad for a while?"

51

"Everyone was at his wake,
then they were all gone,

No one's telling me how
I should carry on.

I'm in this bubble and not
sure how to feel,

I'm trying to be strong whilst
my feelings I conceal."

"Everything's back to normal,
just as it was before:

Mum and Dad chatting about work
and house chores.

Have they forgotten that
Grandad's just died?

Is their grief already over and
have their tears already dried?"

"Go easy on yourself as there's no right way to feel,

You'll have so many emotions, but you will soon start to heal.

One day, the pain will ease and you won't be so sad,

And you will cherish all the time together you had."

"Don't lock up your feelings, you must let them all out,

You're allowed to cry, and scream, and even shout.

Talking is key, so start with the people you trust,

Get it out in the open, you have to, you must."

"Now, go talk to your parents and
remember what I've said,

Keep all the beautiful memories
alive in your head.

Don't be sad that he's gone and
don't feel afraid,

Be glad he was here and cherish
the memories you made."

"Remember I am always with you and your grandad is too,

This time will be tough but you will make it through.

We are with you always, just as I said,

Just breathe and listen to the little voice in your head."

With a small flicker, Big Little Voice disappears,

But I can still hear his voice in my ears.

"If you remember him, your grandad lives on,

But if you forget him, he will really be gone."

I take the box in my hands and walk down the stairs,

To where my parents sit in their comfortable chairs.

Dad's staring into space, as he looks out at the sky,

Mum's wiping her tears as she's starting to cry.

They turn to look as I walk
into the room,

They give a small smile, lifting
the gloom.

"What have you got there?" Mum
says with surprise,

The box has already put some
joy in her eyes.

As **I** open the box and lay
everything on the floor,

The tears start to come and
they eventually pour.

My dad is crying and now
Mum starts to wail,

And **I'm** suddenly thinking this
was a massive fail.

Soon tears subside and they
both sit with me.

Mum says, "What you got here,
come on, let us see?"

We go through the photos,
souvenirs and more,

And they start telling stories
I've never heard before.

Funny stories emerge and
silly tales unfold,

Of my grandad's life, that
had never been told.

So many stories and experiences
that Grandad lived through,

I discovered so much about his
life that I never knew.

The evening is filled with
laughter and tears,

Remembering the wonderful times
we'd had over the years.

Birthdays, Christmases and so
much time spent together,

I will remember that time,
with a smile, forever.

"Wait here," Mum says as she
walks out of the door,

Retrieves a small box and sits
back on the floor.

This was your grandad's watch,
but now it's for you,

Keep it safe or wear it,
if you want to."

"As sad as it is that
Grandad is gone,

You know he was ill, and
he couldn't go on.

We should always be grateful he
was here from the start,

And he'll always be with us in
a space in our heart."

I pick up the boxes and slowly go back up the stair,

Feeling acceptance and hope within the despair.

I will always miss him but I know he's not gone,

He's still with me but in another way from now on.

I look out of the window
and up to the sky,

I wonder if he can see me,
and if it makes him cry.

Is he looking at me with
pride and with joy?

Or is he thinking "Please
don't cry, dear boy."

"Thank you, Grandad," I whisper
as I look into the dark,

For all of the laughing, and
the trips to the park.

The memories we made will
never disappear,

You're always in my heart, so
you'll always be here.

"Big Little Voice, you unravelled
the confusion in my head,

And turned my grief into endless
gratitude instead.

Thank you for being with me
and being my guide,

It's me in the world, with Big Little
Voice by my side."

Acknowledgements

Thank you to my husband and my boys for all their unconditional love and support. You guys never doubted my vision for the Big Little Voice series and I feel so fortunate to have you in my life and very privileged to call you my family. I love you all so much.

Thank you also to Glen Holman, for all your support and perfectly delivering my vision for this book.

This book is hugely personal to me and I dedicate it to my dad who passed away a few years ago. I hope he is as proud of this book as I am and I hope he knows just how much he is missed.

Christine MacDonald is a palliative care nurse who cared for my dad. Thank you so much for giving us a sense of calm at a time when all we felt was panic and fear. Thank you so much for your compassion and your emotional support.

Ria Delahunty-James is a palliative care nurse who also cared for my dad. Thank you for taking the time to sit with my dad and chat with him, for treating him with kindness, compassion and dignity. Your happy disposition really made a huge difference to him at a time which must have been very frightening.

Thank you to all the Big Little Voice readers for your continued kindness and support.

To anyone who has ever lost someone dear to them – please keep the memories of that person alive because those wonderful memories, that live in your heart, can never be taken away from you.

x

About the Author

M.G. Vaciago is the author of the Big Little Voice series, books written to inspire and empower children and young adults. The first books in the series, Big Little Voice Colours the Grey and Big Little Voice Behind the Smile, did exactly that and she received many positive reviews. She is currently working on the next books in the series which will be released in the near future. When she is not writing, M.G. also provides author visits in schools, as well as delivering workshops.

M.G. Vaciago can be found at
www.mgvaciago.com

About the Illustrator

Glen Holman is an internationally renowned illustrator and book designer whose work has been exhibited in London as well as appearing on Netflix. His life-long passion for illustration started from the moment he held a pencil and has led to the creation of hundreds of books and countless pieces of art. Glen's greatest quality is undoubtedly his intrepid canine companion and noble steed, Winston, the true puppeteer of Glen's success.

Glen can be found at glenholman.com or on Instagram @g.a.holman.

From the Author of Big Little Voice Colour the Grey

Big Little Voice

BEHIND THE SMILE

By M.G. Vaciago   Illustrated by Glen Holman

Beth suffers terribly with low self-esteem, believing her friends are prettier, smarter and happier than she is. One night, a Big Little Voice appears to her and takes her on a trip to see first-hand the reality that was hiding behind the smiles.

When you realise the prettiest smiles are hiding the biggest secrets, be the one person that puts a genuine smile on their face.

Join Beth on her incredible journey, see the world that hides behind the smiles of those closest to her. Meet Big Little Voice and realise that the most beautiful thing in the world is being uniquely and unashamedly yourself!

Big Little Voice
COLOURS
THE **Grey**

By M.G. Vaciago   Illustrated by
                        Glen Holman

'Why me?' Tommy would ask. After being relentlessly bullied at school for a number of years Tommy is now completely withdrawn from everyone and everything he once loved. That is, until, one night when his Big Little Voice appears to him and takes him on a journey to a reality he never could have imagined...

Join Tommy on his incredible journey, see the world through his eyes and experience what he feels. Meet Big Little Voice and uncover a side to bullying as you've never seen before and realise your inner superhero was within you all along.